P9-DDY-724

C

Learning to Read, Step by Step!

Ready to Read   Preschool–Kindergarten
• big type and easy words • rhyme and rhythm • picture clues
For children who know the alphabet and are eager to
begin reading.

Reading with Help   Preschool–Grade 1
• basic vocabulary • short sentences • simple stories
For children who recognize familiar words and sound out
new words with help.

Reading on Your Own   Grades 1–3
• engaging characters • easy-to-follow plots • popular topics
For children who are ready to read on their own.

Reading Paragraphs   Grades 2–3
• challenging vocabulary • short paragraphs • exciting stories
For newly independent readers who read simple sentences
with confidence.

Ready for Chapters   Grades 2–4
• chapters • longer paragraphs • full-color art
For children who want to take the plunge into chapter books
but still like colorful pictures.

STEP INTO READING® is designed to give every child a successful
reading experience. The grade levels are only guides; children will progress
through the steps at their own speed, developing confidence in their reading.

Remember, a lifetime love of reading starts with a single step!

*The editors would like to thank Jim Breheny, Director, Bronx Zoo, and EVP of WCS Zoos &
Aquarium, New York, for his assistance in the preparation of this book.*

Visit us on the Web!
StepIntoReading.com
randomhousekids.com

Educators and librarians, for a variety of teaching tools, visit us at
RHTeachersLibrarians.com

ISBN 978-1-101-93901-7 (trade) — ISBN 978-1-101-93902-4 (lib. bdg.) —
ISBN 978-1-101-93903-1 (ebook)

Printed in the United States of America
10 9 8 7 6 5 4 3 2 1

WILD KRATTS®

Wild Insects and Spiders!

by Martin Kratt and Chris Kratt

Random House 🏠 New York

Hey, it's us,
the Kratt Brothers—
Martin and Chris!
And we love insects
and spiders.

"You mean like the bee
on my face?" Martin asks.
"Exactly!" Chris says.

Insects have six legs.
They have three body
parts: a head, a thorax,
and an abdomen.

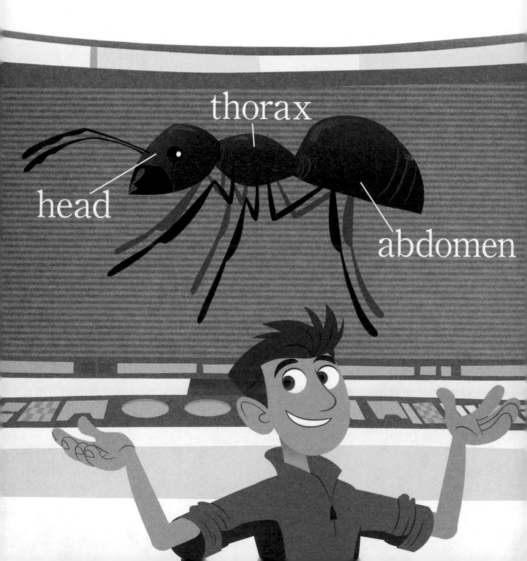

6 7 8

5

1

head

4 2

3

Weaver Spider

Spiders have eight legs.

They are arachnids,

not insects.

Dragonfly!

Dragonflies have been
around since the time
of the dinosaurs.

They can fly forward,
backward, and even
upside down!
"It's a great flying power!"
says Martin.

Dragonflies are predators.
They use their flying
powers to catch insects
right out of the air.

But they can also be prey.
Baby alligators love
to eat dragonflies.
"Watch out!" Chris says.

Mosquito!

Mosquitoes survive by sucking the blood of animals, including humans!

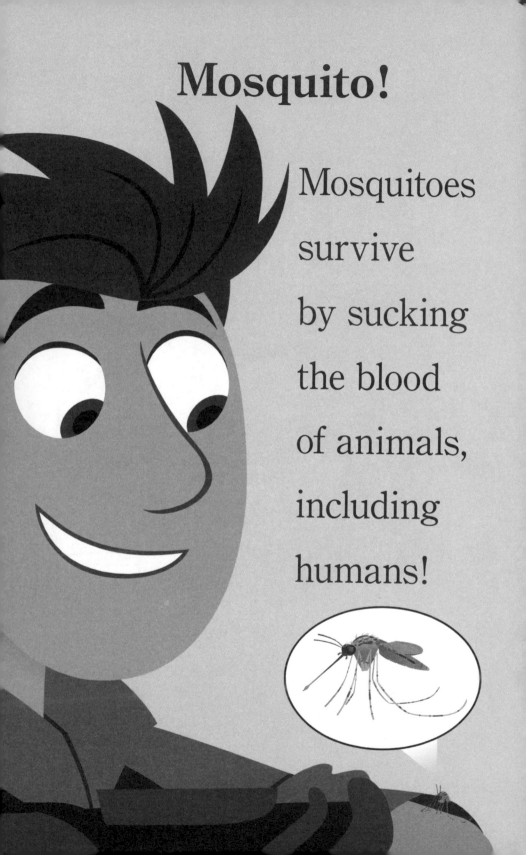

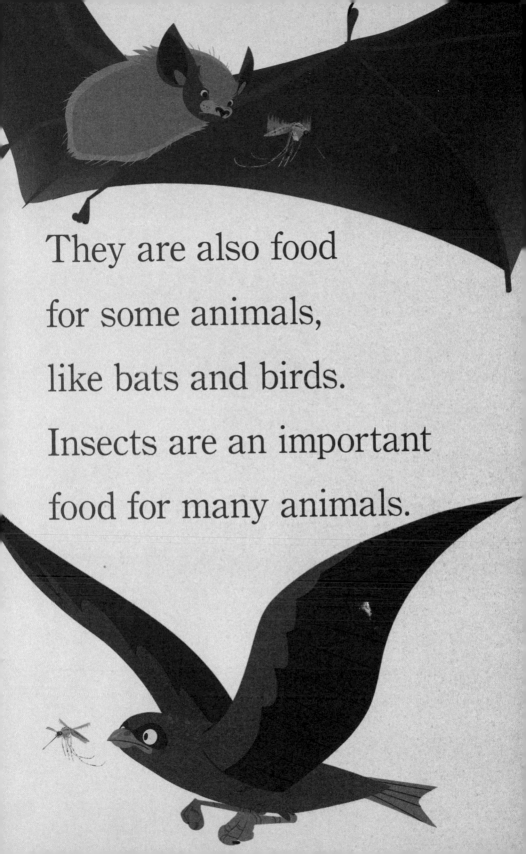

They are also food
for some animals,
like bats and birds.
Insects are an important
food for many animals.

Monarch Butterfly!

Butterflies are strong fliers.
Some can fly
thousands of miles.

But like many insects, they have to crawl before they can fly. "I'm not flying yet," says Martin.

The Butterfly Life Cycle!

First an egg is laid,
and a caterpillar hatches.
After eating lots of leaves,
it makes a cocoon around
itself—the pupa stage.

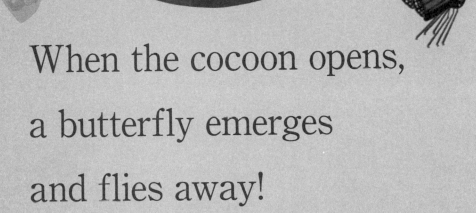

When the cocoon opens,
a butterfly emerges
and flies away!

egg   caterpillar

butterfly   pupa

Praying Mantis!

The praying mantis has
special legs to catch its prey.
When prey comes near,
the mantis grabs it.

A large praying mantis
can even catch
hummingbirds!
"I'm out
of here!"
Chris says.

19

Honeybee!

Honeybees are
hard workers.
They collect nectar
from flowers.
This is food for their hive.
Thousands of bees
live in a single hive!

Bees have to be careful.
Predators like the crab spider
hide in the flowers
to catch them.

Golden Orb Spider!

Many spiders make webs
to catch their prey.
The sticky webs are strong
and hard to see.

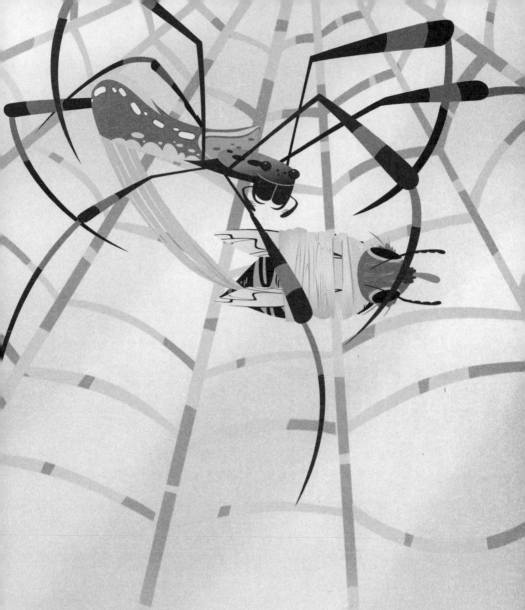

When an insect gets stuck
in the web, the spider kills it
and wraps it up to eat later!

"There are over one million kinds of insects and spiders!" Chris says.

"We've got lots more insect adventuring to do!" Martin adds.

Go, Creature Powers!